109

P9-DYP-163

Lexile: _____ 370 L _____

AR/BL: _____ 2.3 _____

AR Points: _____ 0.5 _____

THE NICE CLEAN PARK

Written by Joanne Meier and Cecilia Minden • Illustrated by Bob Ostrom
Created by Herbie J. Thorpe

ABOUT THE AUTHORS

Joanne Meier, PhD, has worked as an elementary school teacher, university professor, and researcher. She earned her BA in early childhood education from the University of South Carolina, and her MEd and PhD in education from the University of Virginia. She currently works as a literacy consultant for schools and private organizations. Joanne lives in Virginia with her husband Eric, daughters Kella and Erin, two cats, and a gerbil.

Cecilia Minden, PhD, is the former director of the Language and Literacy Program at the Harvard Graduate School of Education. She is now a reading consultant for school and library publications. She earned her PhD in reading education from the University of Virginia. Cecilia and her husband, Dave Cupp, live outside Chapel Hill, North Carolina. They enjoy sharing their love of reading with their grandchildren, Chelsea and Qadir.

ABOUT THE ILLUSTRATOR

Bob Ostrom has been illustrating children's books for nearly twenty years. A graduate of the New England School of Art & Design at Suffolk University, Bob has worked for such companies as Disney, Nickelodeon, and Cartoon Network. He lives in North Carolina with his wife Melissa and three children, Will, Charlie, and Mae.

ABOUT THE SERIES CREATOR

Herbie J. Thorpe had long envisioned a beginning-readers' series about a fun, energetic bear with a big imagination. Herbie is a book lover and an avid supporter of libraries and the role they play in fostering the love of reading. He consults with librarians and matches them with the perfect books for their students and patrons. He lives in Louisiana with his wife Misty and their daughter Carson.

The Child's World®

Published in the United States of America by The Child's World®
1980 Lookout Drive • Mankato, MN 56003-1705
800-599-READ • www.childsworld.com

Acknowledgments
The Child's World®: Mary Berendes, Publishing Director
The Design Lab: Kathleen Petelinsek, Design;
Kari Tobin, Page Production
Artistic Assistant: Richard Carbajal

Library of Congress Cataloging-in-Publication Data
Meier, Joanne D.
  The nice clean park / by Joanne Meier and Cecilia Minden ;
illustrated by Bob Ostrom.
     p. cm. — (Herbster readers)
  ISBN 978-1-60253-213-7 (library bound : alk. paper)
  [1. Parks—Fiction. 2. Bears—Fiction.] I. Minden, Cecilia. II. Ostrom,
Bob, ill. III. Title. IV. Series.

PZ7.M5148Nic 2009
[E]—dc22   2009004000

Herbie Bear was busy drawing.
He had some great ideas.

"What are you drawing, Herbie?" asked Mom.

"A special machine," explained Herbie. "It's my very own invention. I think it could really work!"

"This is called the Park Picker-Upper.
It cleans up places where people play!"

"I thought of it after we went to the park yesterday. The mess there made it hard to have much fun."

"My invention has a big scoop on the front for picking up trash. It puts the trash right into the trash can."

"This claw over here plants beautiful trees and flowers. It can even pull weeds!"

"This arm has screwdrivers and wrenches. It repairs broken equipment."

"The back of my machine has a big broom.
It sweeps up pebbles and sticks from the
basketball court."

"Wow, Herbie!" said Mom. "That's a great invention. I was thinking about the messy park, too."

Mom smiled. "I have my own invention," she said. "It's called Park Clean-Up Day. Let's go!"

The Bear family gathered supplies
and headed to the park.

"You're right, Herbie," said Hannah.
"This park does need a good cleaning."

The Bear family got right to work.
Everyone had a job to do.

Mom put on some gloves and started collecting trash.

Hannah put on gloves, too. She planted bright flowers near the bike path.

She planted more over by the picnic tables.

Dad went to work near the swings. The wood chips underneath had been kicked and spread all over. Dad raked them until they were smooth.

After that, he tightened up the monkey bars.
A few of the bars were really loose!

Hank used a broom to clean up the basketball court.
He swept up lots of pebbles and sticks.

He even found a quarter!
Mom said he could keep it.

"Hey look!" said Herbie. "Here comes Michael and his family!"

"We got your phone message," said Michael's dad.
"We came to help clean the park, too. It's a great idea!"

With all the extra hands, the work went much faster. Everyone had fun pitching in to help. After a while, they all stopped to rest.

Michael's parents had brought a great surprise—a picnic lunch!

Everyone munched happily on sandwiches and chips.
They had cold lemonade and watermelon.

When everyone had finished, they cleaned up their picnic area. Then it was time to head home.

The next day, Herbie was drawing again.
"What are you drawing this time, Herbie?"
asked Mom.

"Another invention," explained Herbie.
"It's called Helping Hands."

Herbie and Mom just smiled.